The Magic Pencil and Me

A.M. ALsalih

AuthorHouse™
1663 Liberty Drive
Bloomington, IN 47403
www.authorhouse.com
Phone: 1 (800) 839-8640

This book is printed on acid-free paper.

ISBN: 978-1-7283-3342-7 (sc)
ISBN: 978-1-7283-3343-4 (e)

Library of Congress Control Number: 2019917268

Print information available on the last page.

Published by AuthorHouse 10/29/2019

authorHOUSE

The Magic Pencil and Me

Hi everyone. My name is Youssif. I enjoy reading books from all over the world. I have a big shelf full of books, and have read them all.

My problem is that I don't like to write. My mom tried to help me learn to write the alphabet, but I didn't like it, so I hid my pencil under my bed.

One day while I was reading, a storm blew in. A big wind took all of the letters off the pages of my books and carried them out the window.

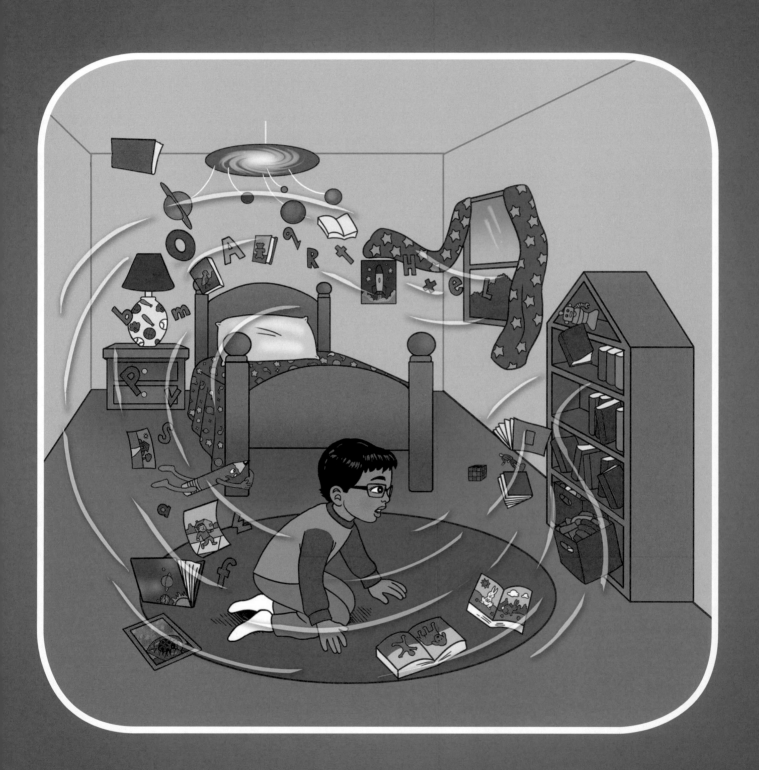

At first, I trembled in fear when I found my books emptied of all their wonderful stories. I felt so sad because I had nothing to read any more, so I hid under my bed and cried.

At that moment, my pencil started to move and talk to me.

"Youssif," said the pencil.

"Are you talking?" I said.

"Yes," said the pencil.

"You know my name?" I said.

"Yes, and I know how sad you are," the pencil said.

"You are right. All of my books are empty," I said.

"Don't worry. I can help you," the pencil said.

"How can you help me?" I asked in wonder.

"Just pick me up and hold me," the pencil said, "and together, we will write all the stories again."

"But I don't know how to write."

"Just hold me. I promise to help you."

When I held the pencil and looked at it, it asked me, "Which book would you like to rewrite first?"

I looked at all my empty books and said, "Space! I remember everything about this book. It's my favorite one."

"Let's start," said the pencil.

We wrote the title of the book first, and then word after word, page after page followed. When we finished, we chose another book and another book, until we had done all of them.

Then, my pencil and I wrote this story.

I'm thrilled that you are reading it now. Maybe you can write a story too!

ABOUT THE AUTHOR

Raising three autistic children provides endless real life experiences. The author takes the challenges faced at school or in public and builds a story that provides a solution.

A.M. AL-SALIH's stories are a bedtime ritual that has resulted in noticeable behaviour improvements with her kids. It is her hope that sharing these stories with the world will give other parents the chance to support their young ones in achieving positive lives.

Printed in the United States
By Bookmasters